Goldie at the Orphanage

Martha Sandwall-Bergström

Illustrated by Eva Stålsjö

Floris Books

First published in Swedish as
Kulla-Gulla på barnhemmet
by Albert Bonniers, Stockholm in 1986

Text © Martha Sandwell-Bergström 1986
Illustrations © Eva Stålsjö 1986
English version © Floris Books 2004

First published in English in 2004 by
Floris Books, 15 Harrison Gardens, Edinburgh
British Library CIP Data available
ISBN 0-86315-443-3
Printed in Belgium

One night many years ago, an unknown boat was wrecked off the Swedish coast. When dawn came, pieces of wreckage were floating on the waves, among them a basket tied to a plank. A fisherman went out in his boat to see what it was.

"There's a child in the basket," he shouted back to the shore. "I think it's still alive." The fisherman pulled the basket in to land and one of the women took care of the rescued child.

The child was a pretty little girl, just a few months old. But none of the fishing folk could afford to keep her. They had to hand her over to the nearest orphanage.

"Her name is embroidered on her clothes," said the fisherman's wife who took the child. "It's Geraldine Beatrice Frederika. The blankets in the basket are so fine, we think she must be from a noble family."

"Here, everyone is treated the same," said the superintendent, "and that name is much too long. We'll call her Goldie."

So she was called Goldie. The name suited the little girl very well because of her golden locks. The years passed, and Goldie grew into a nice quiet child. It was seldom she got punished or had to stand in the corner, which the children in the orphanage were made to do when they were disobedient.

By the rules all the girls had to wear their hair in pigtails so that they would look neat and tidy. Every morning there was much crying and screaming when their hair was brushed and straightened.

Goldie's hair was so fine, it was one of the most difficult to do.

"Stand still," said the nursemaid who was brushing Goldie's hair. "Nobody has such difficult hair as you!" She pulled Goldie's hair back and tied it so hard that it hurt. Goldie's eyes filled with tears but she tried not to cry.

The nursemaid bent and gave Goldie a kiss to comfort her.

"Your hair is beautiful," she said, "but it's impossible to brush."

When Goldie was about six, a new girl called Lotta arrived from another orphanage. Like Goldie, she had been found as a baby, abandoned in a box outside the place where she had lived before.

Goldie and Lotta became good friends at once and were always together. They had no toys but they thought up all sorts of games to play.

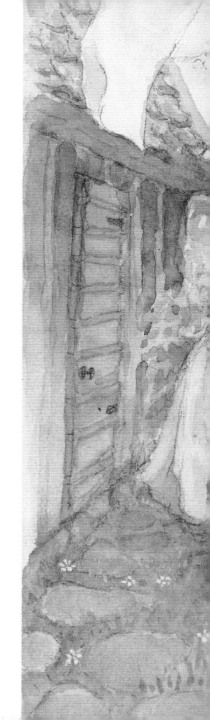

Every week in the orphanage, the children had to help at washing and cleaning. The floors had to be scrubbed, the windows cleaned and everything dusted. The clothes were washed in a big pot in the yard, then rinsed under the cold pump. Goldie and Lotta took turns outside at pumping the water. It was hard work and they would finish the day very tired.

At night they shared the same bed, and when everybody was asleep, they would lie and whisper quietly to each other. They often imagined what their mothers were like.

"I'm sure my mother was very kind," said Goldie. "When the boat sank, she didn't think of saving herself, but only of rescuing me."

"My mother was so poor she couldn't afford to keep me," said Lotta, "though I'm sure she really wanted to."

One of the girls, Mia, caught a bad fever on a washing day in midwinter. She coughed a lot and had to stay in bed a long time. Sometimes Lotta would smuggle in a little kitten that she had found outside and secretly looked after. It was forbidden, but Mia though it was such fun to play with the cat.

One day they played a game where they hid the kitten under Mia's blankets and all three girls said mia-mia together so that it sounded just like miaow-miaow. Then the kitten jumped out from under the blankets, and suddenly dashed across the floor and away.

Another girl saw the little animal and shouted: "Lotta has the kitten again!"

All the children rushed after the cat to catch it, but it took fright and ran about all over the place with the girls in pursuit. Everybody joined in, including one of the nursemaids who picked up a broom and ran after it.

A few boys were making matchsticks, which were used for lighting the fire. In the confusion they knocked over the can of sulphur, which was extremely poisonous. The sulphur poured out in a chocolate-brown stream, and a little chap suddenly crept forward to taste the deadly mixture. One of the nursemaids managed to save him at the last moment.

"This is all your fault," said the nursemaid sternly, as she finally shooed the cat out of the door with the broom. Lotta, who was the most to blame, was beaten with the rod on her hand. Goldie got off with having to sit in the corner.

As further punishment they had to scrub a whole floor by themselves. That was a really hard chore for such little girls.

Lotta and Goldie were now seven years old, and in those days old enough to start work. Every year there was an auction of orphans. Anybody who needed cheap help could buy a boy or a girl in return for giving the child a home and a little food. It was easier to place the girls in a home than the boys. Girls ate less and they could work outside as well as helping with the household chores.

Goldie and Lotta and three other children were taken to the auction house where there was a line of carriages and horse-wagons waiting outside. Lots of people, mainly poor farmers, had come to find cheap labour by taking on a foster-child.

Inside the auction room, the children were put in front of a
platform where a man sat at a table. He was the auctioneer.
The children looked fearfully at the crowd of "buyers."
Where would they end up? Would they be lucky and find
someone who would look after them well, or would they
have to work hard and hardly be fed and
perhaps be beaten for the slightest thing?
They had heard about these things.

The man at the table pointed at Lotta.

"You there, come here and climb up on the stool," he said. Lotta became frightened, and her lower lip trembled. Goldie squeezed her hand to give her courage. The man on the podium looked sternly at her and Lotta climbed up on the stool. Then a large lady with a plumed hat and fancy coat stepped forward and examined her, while Lotta closed her eyes tightly.

"I'll take her," she heard the lady say. "She's a little short, but she can stand on a stool when she's washing the dishes. She can eat as much food as she wants with us. Lots of work and lots of food! We have an inn."

Then the auctioneer's club hit the table with a bang that decided Lotta's fate for many years to come.

Through a veil of tears, Goldie saw Lotta being taken out of the room.

"Oh, if only I had been allowed to go with her," thought Goldie. Now it was her turn and she climbed bravely up on the stool. Everybody looked at her, and she felt she was going to cry. She heard a voice, as in a dream, say: "I'll take her."

Terrified, Goldie looked up into a hairy, unshaven face. But the man smiled in a friendly way and said: "I think you'll make a fine little nursemaid. We have lots of small children, you know. And you'll have to milk the cows as well, but we'll teach you that by and by."

Goldie went with the man, who was now her master, to a simple horse-wagon parked outside in the yard. His name was Hermansson and he was a small farmer. He had to sell a few piglets before they could leave. Goldie was told to climb up into the wagon and wait.

"It'll take a while, but there's some food here if you get a bit hungry!" He took a round loaf of bread and a piece of sausage and cut slices with his knife for Goldie and himself.

At the other side of the yard, Goldie noticed that Lotta was climbing up into a very fancy carriage, a light pony-trap with two big red wheels, and shiny brasses on the horse's harness. The only seat was taken up by the man who held the reins and the large woman. Lotta had to climb on at the back and hold tightly so she wouldn't fall off.

"How I wish Lotta had come with me instead," thought Goldie.

The pony-trap from the inn came right past Goldie as she
waited in the horse-wagon. Goldie waved eagerly.

"Lotta!" she shouted. But Lotta couldn't wave back.
She was holding on with both hands so as not to fall off.
But she looked back, and Goldie saw she was crying.

Goldie waved for a long time after her playmate from
the orphanage. "Shall we ever meet again?" she asked
herself sadly.

to be continued in *Goldie at the Farm...*